W9-BRH-741

Disney's
Princess Magic

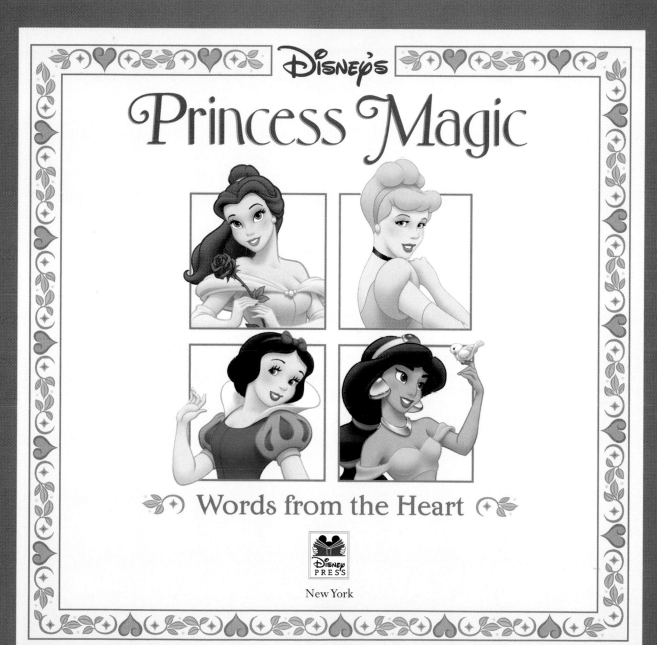

Words from the Heart

DISNEY
PRESS

New York

For information address Disney Press,

114 Fifth Avenue, New York, New York 10011-5690.

First Edition

3 5 7 9 10 8 6 4 2

Library of Congress Catalog Card Number: 2001086036

ISBN 0-7868-3296-7

Printed in the United States of America

Designed by Cathy L. Colbert

Cover designed by Angela Corbo Gier

For more Disney Press fun, visit www.disneybooks.com

Contents

Princess magic isn't just

about beautiful gowns,

dreams come true, and

happily ever after . . .

. . . although your favorite Disney princess stories certainly do contain a healthy dose of *that* kind of magic. But there is another, more understated kind of magic that the princess stories embody so well. It's the kind that can be found in living life to the very fullest—believing in yourself, seeing the good in those around you, and seizing the day. So read on and feel the magic in this collection of inspirational, funny, and just plain memorable quotations from your favorite Disney princess films. Included are thoughtful words from Cinderella, Jasmine, Belle, and their friends, as well as nonroyal Disney heroines like Mulan, the Blue Fairy, Alice, and Pocahontas. Which just goes to show: you don't have to be royalty to discover the princess magic in your own life.

PRINCESS MAGIC

The Glass
Is
Half Full

PRINCESS MAGIC

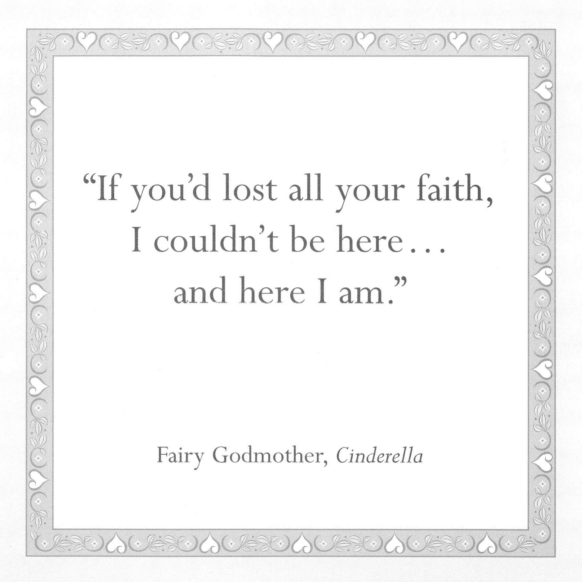

"If you'd lost all your faith,
I couldn't be here ...
and here I am."

Fairy Godmother, *Cinderella*

PRINCESS MAGIC

"This ain't going to be pretty, but don't worry. Things will work out."

Mushu, *Mulan*

PRINCESS MAGIC

"Give yourself some time.
You're still a seed."

Flik, *A Bug's Life*

PRINCESS MAGIC

"She can't be *all* bad."

Fauna (on Maleficent), *Sleeping Beauty*

PRINCESS MAGIC

"That's our lot in life.
It's not a lot,
but it's our life."

The Queen, *A Bug's Life*

PRINCESS MAGIC

"A ray of hope there still may be, in this gift I give to thee."

Merryweather, *Sleeping Beauty*

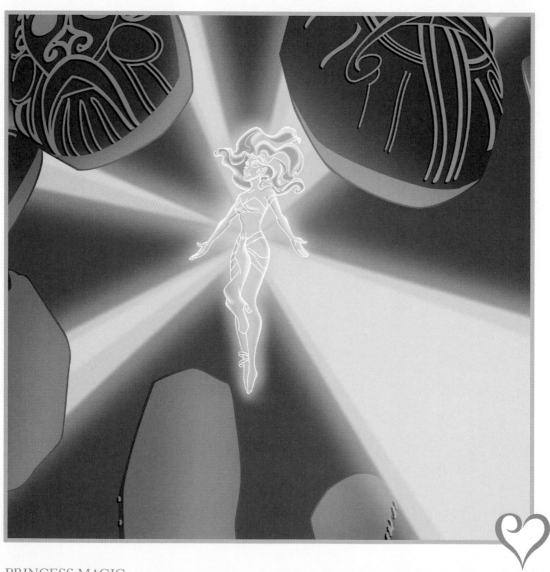

PRINCESS MAGIC

"All will be well....
Be not afraid."

Princess Kida, *Atlantis*

PRINCESS MAGIC

Put Your Best Foot Forward

PRINCESS MAGIC

"Look up, speak nicely, and don't twiddle your fingers."

Queen of Hearts, *Alice in Wonderland*

PRINCESS MAGIC

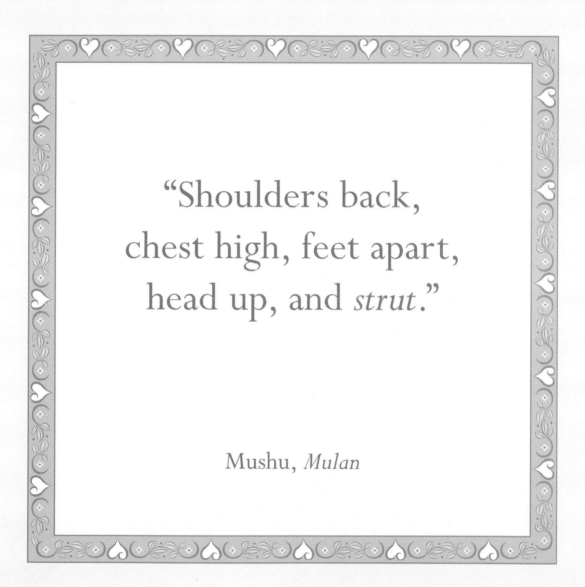

"Shoulders back,
chest high, feet apart,
head up, and *strut*."

Mushu, *Mulan*

PRINCESS MAGIC

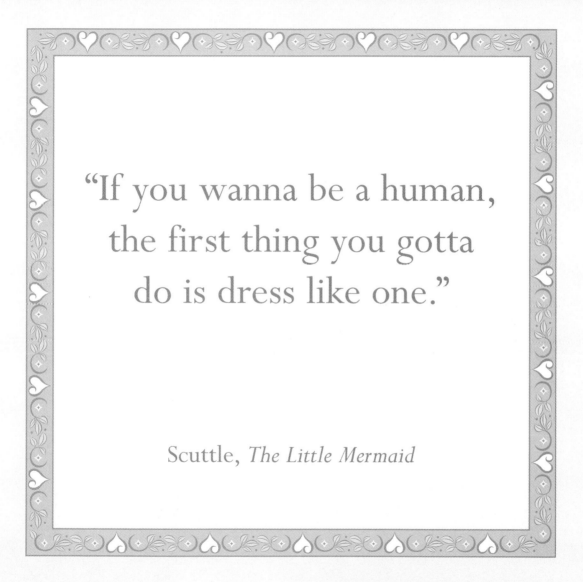

"If you wanna be a human, the first thing you gotta do is dress like one."

Scuttle, *The Little Mermaid*

PRINCESS MAGIC

"Above all ... you must control your temper."

Mrs. Potts, *Beauty and the Beast*

PRINCESS MAGIC

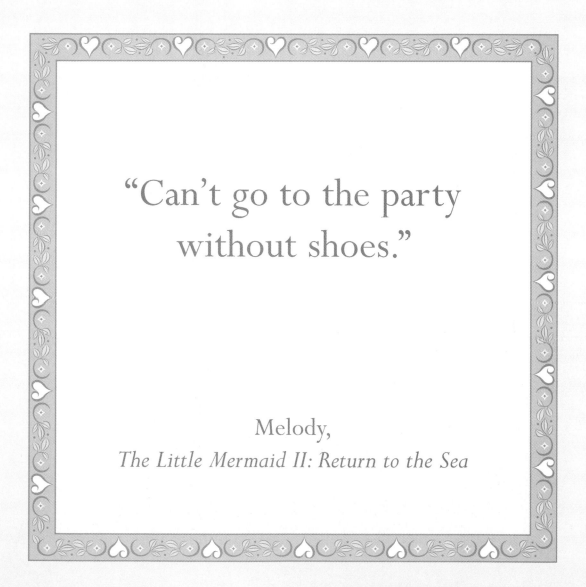

"Can't go to the party
without shoes."

Melody,
The Little Mermaid II: Return to the Sea

PRINCESS MAGIC

"Just do your best, dear."

Fauna, *Sleeping Beauty*

PUT YOUR BEST FOOT FORWARD

PRINCESS MAGIC

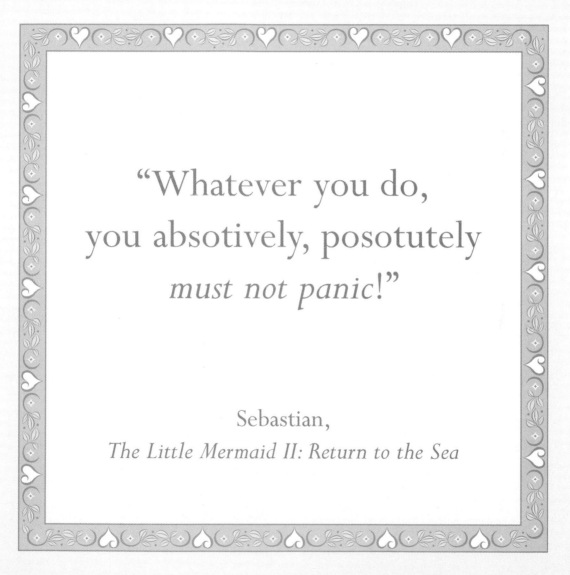

"Whatever you do,
you absotively, posotutely
must not panic!"

Sebastian,
The Little Mermaid II: Return to the Sea

PRINCESS MAGIC

Confidence
Is Key

"Just be confident.
You'll be fine."

The Queen, *A Bug's Life*

CONFIDENCE IS KEY

"I'm a big tough girl.
I tie my own sandals
and everything."

Megara, *Hercules*

PRINCESS MAGIC

"If you want something done, you got to do it yourself."

Sebastian, *The Little Mermaid*

PRINCESS MAGIC

"I'm a fast learner."

Princess Jasmine, *Aladdin*

CONFIDENCE IS KEY

PRINCESS MAGIC

"Remember
who you are."

Mufasa, *The Lion King*

PRINCESS MAGIC

"If humans can do it,
so can we."

Flora, *Sleeping Beauty*

PRINCESS MAGIC

Listen
to Your
Heart

PRINCESS MAGIC

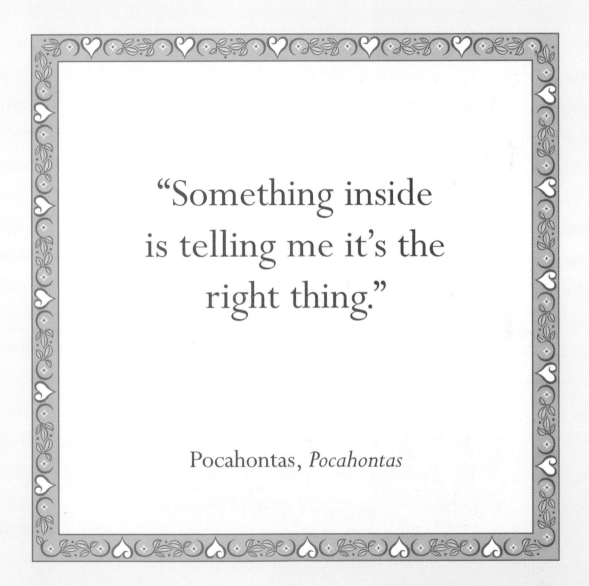

"Something inside
is telling me it's the
right thing."

Pocahontas, *Pocahontas*

PRINCESS MAGIC

"I was just
giving myself some
good advice."

Alice, *Alice in Wonderland*

PRINCESS MAGIC

"Always let
your conscience be
your guide."

Blue Fairy, *Pinocchio*

PRINCESS MAGIC

"Reflect before you act."

Mulan, *Mulan*

LISTEN TO YOUR HEART

PRINCESS MAGIC

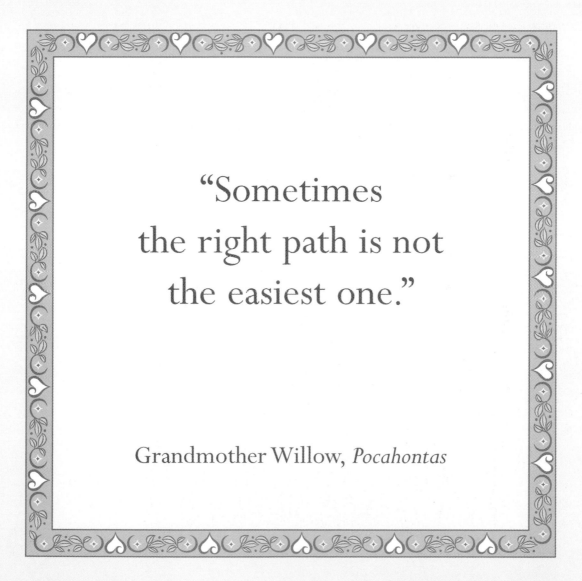

"Sometimes
the right path is not
the easiest one."

Grandmother Willow, *Pocahontas*

PRINCESS MAGIC

Family and Friends Are There for You

PRINCESS MAGIC

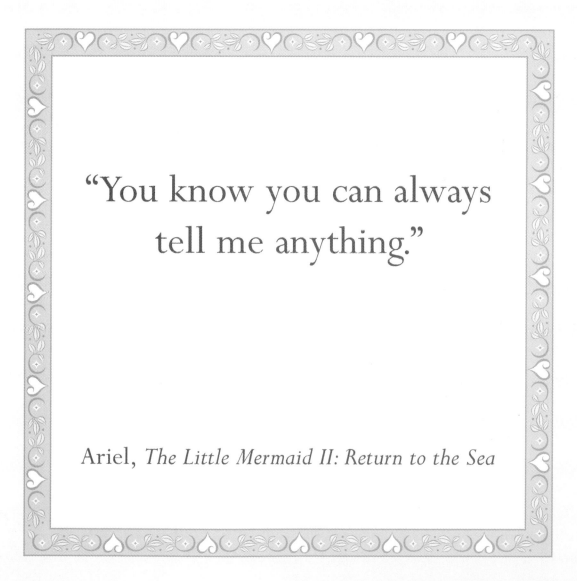

"You know you can always tell me anything."

Ariel, *The Little Mermaid II: Return to the Sea*

FAMILY AND FRIENDS ARE THERE FOR YOU

PRINCESS MAGIC

"Look at us!
We're a complete set!"

Jessie, *Toy Story 2*

FAMILY AND FRIENDS ARE THERE FOR YOU

PRINCESS MAGIC

"Don't be afraid.
We're right behind you."

Doc, *Snow White*

FAMILY AND FRIENDS ARE THERE FOR YOU

PRINCESS MAGIC

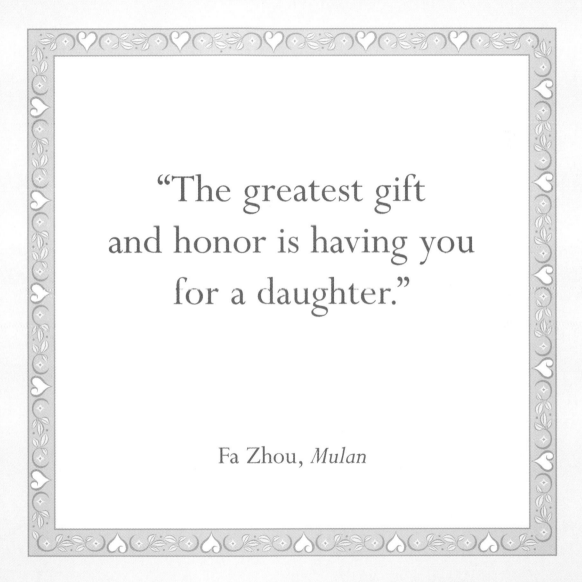

"The greatest gift
and honor is having you
for a daughter."

Fa Zhou, *Mulan*

FAMILY AND FRIENDS ARE THERE FOR YOU

PRINCESS MAGIC

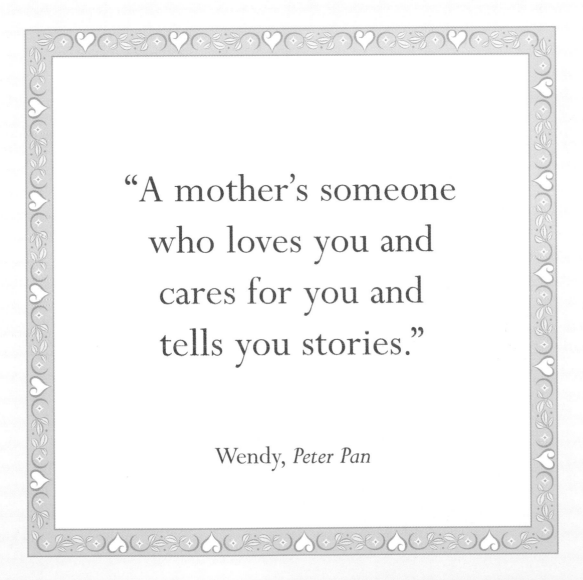

"A mother's someone
who loves you and
cares for you and
tells you stories."

Wendy, *Peter Pan*

PRINCESS MAGIC

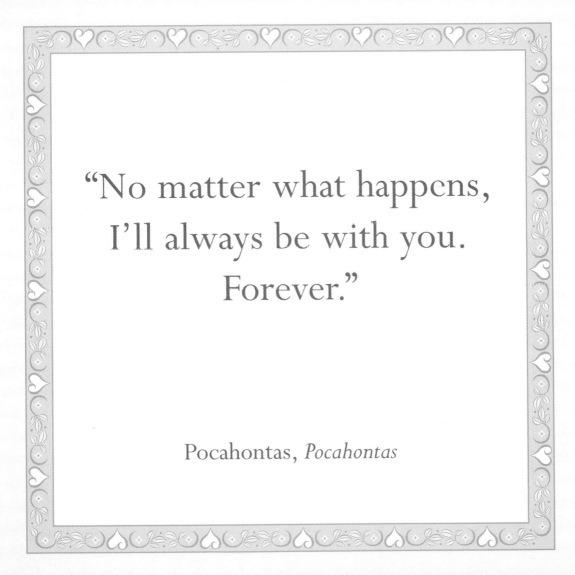

"No matter what happens,
I'll always be with you.
Forever."

Pocahontas, *Pocahontas*

PRINCESS MAGIC

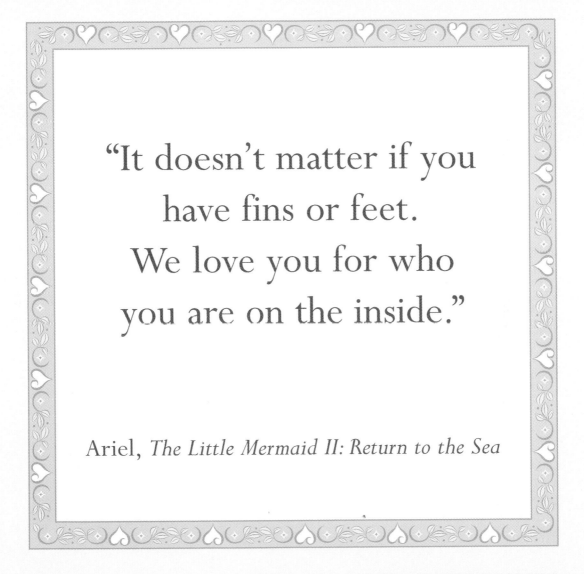

"It doesn't matter if you have fins or feet. We love you for who you are on the inside."

Ariel, *The Little Mermaid II: Return to the Sea*

FAMILY AND FRIENDS ARE THERE FOR YOU

PRINCESS MAGIC

A Little Imagination Goes a Long Way

PRINCESS MAGIC

"I'm making this up as I go."

Mulan, *Mulan*

A LITTLE IMAGINATION GOES A LONG WAY

PRINCESS MAGIC

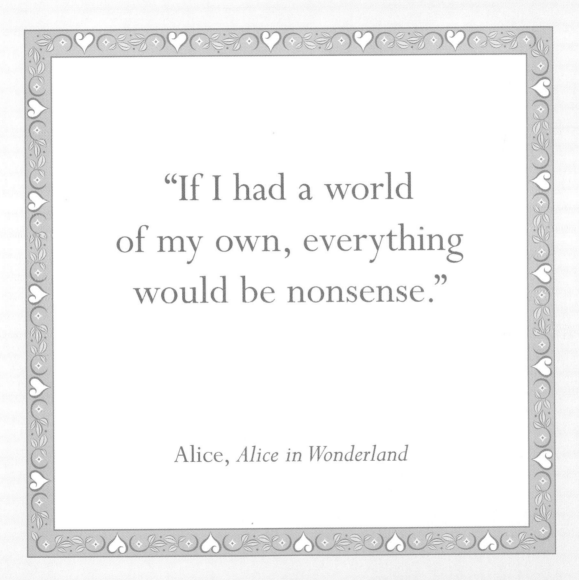

"If I had a world of my own, everything would be nonsense."

Alice, *Alice in Wonderland*

PRINCESS MAGIC

"Sometimes I even
pretend I have fins!"

Melody,
The Little Mermaid II: Return to the Sea

A LITTLE IMAGINATION GOES A LONG WAY

PRINCESS MAGIC

"Some people use imagination."

Belle, *Beauty and the Beast*

PRINCESS MAGIC

"Pretend it's a seed, okay?"

Princess Dot, *A Bug's Life*

A LITTLE IMAGINATION GOES A LONG WAY

PRINCESS MAGIC

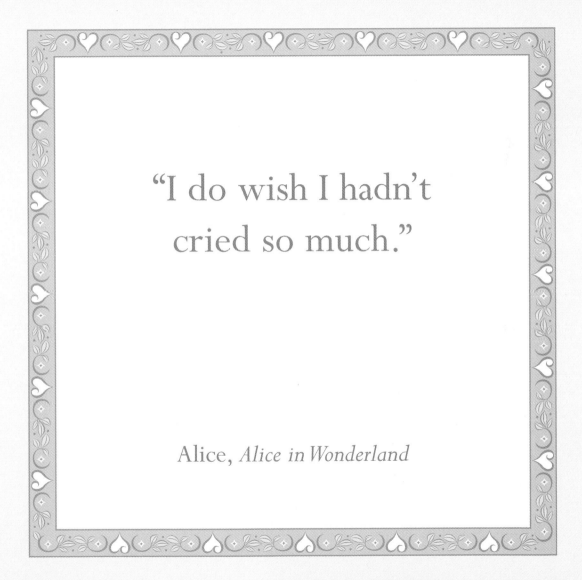

"I do wish I hadn't
cried so much."

Alice, *Alice in Wonderland*

Looks
Can Be
Deceiving

PRINCESS MAGIC

"He's really kind
and gentle."

Belle, *Beauty and the Beast*

PRINCESS MAGIC

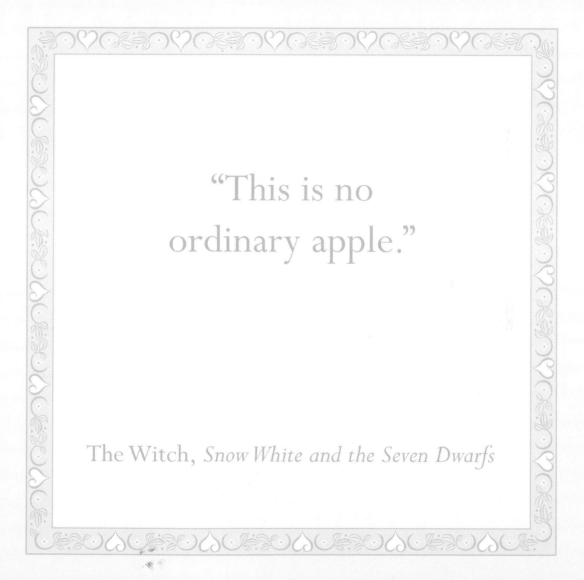

"This is no ordinary apple."

The Witch, *Snow White and the Seven Dwarfs*

LOOKS CAN BE DECEIVING

PRINCESS MAGIC

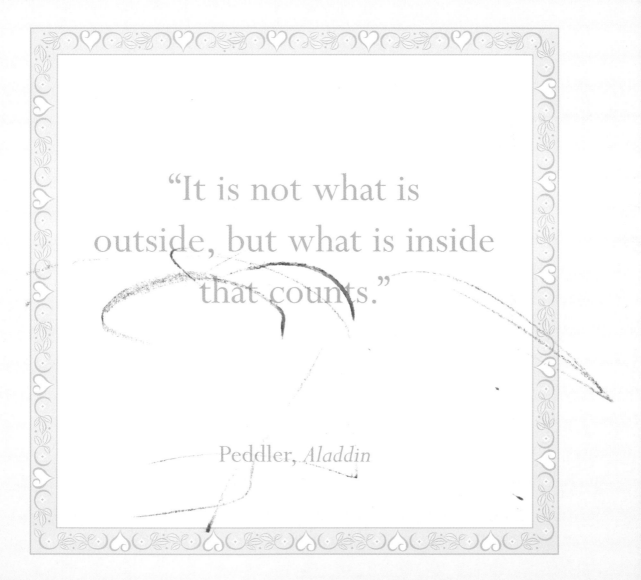

"It is not what is outside, but what is inside that counts."

Peddler, *Aladdin*

PRINCESS MAGIC

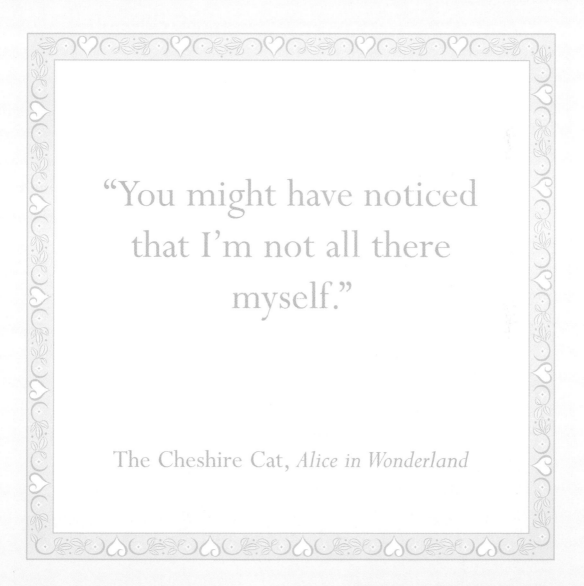

"You might have noticed that I'm not all there myself."

The Cheshire Cat, *Alice in Wonderland*

LOOKS CAN BE DECEIVING

PRINCESS MAGIC

Be Your
Own
Person

PRINCESS MAGIC

"You got a lot
of spunk."

The Queen, *A Bug's Life*

PRINCESS MAGIC

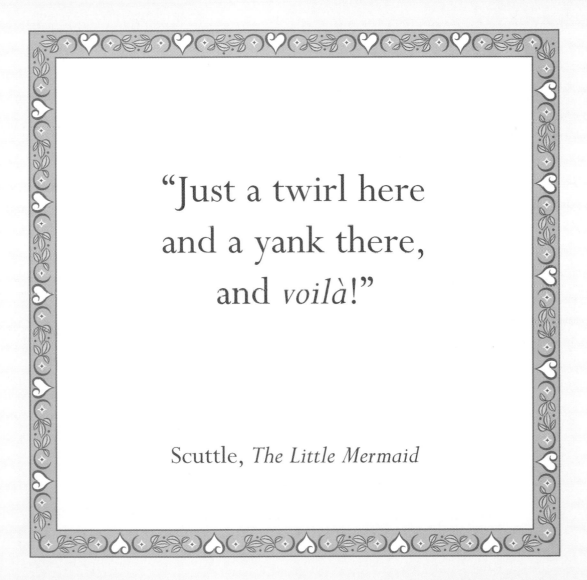

"Just a twirl here
and a yank there,
and *voilà*!"

Scuttle, *The Little Mermaid*

PRINCESS MAGIC

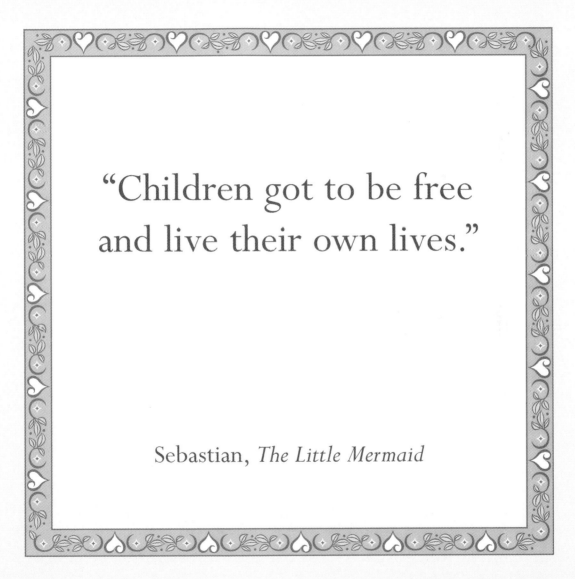

"Children got to be free and live their own lives."

Sebastian, *The Little Mermaid*

PRINCESS MAGIC

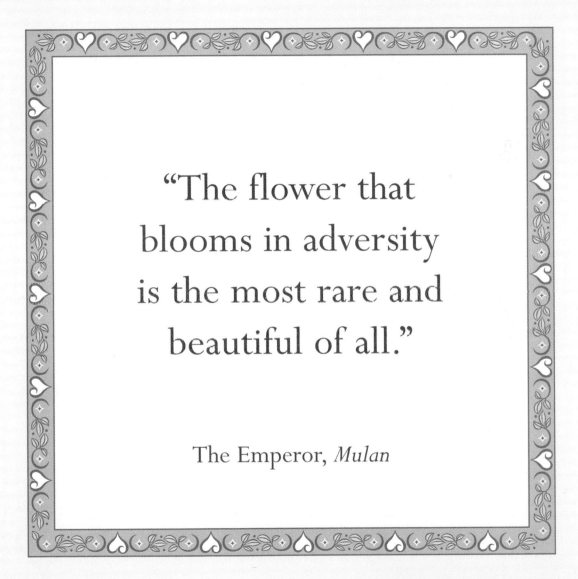

"The flower that
blooms in adversity
is the most rare and
beautiful of all."

The Emperor, *Mulan*

PRINCESS MAGIC

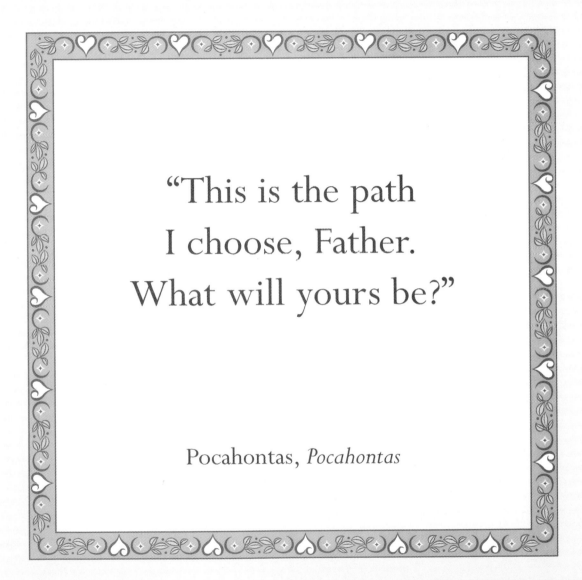

"This is the path
I choose, Father.
What will yours be?"

Pocahontas, *Pocahontas*

PRINCESS MAGIC

Give Peace
a Chance

PRINCESS MAGIC

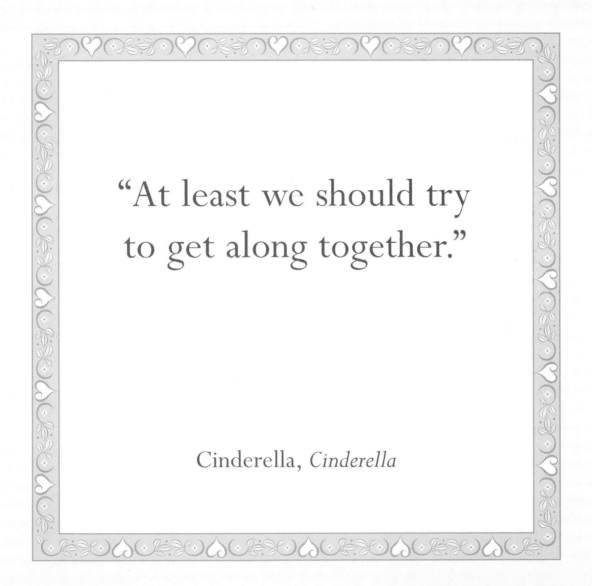

"At least we should try
to get along together."

Cinderella, *Cinderella*

PRINCESS MAGIC

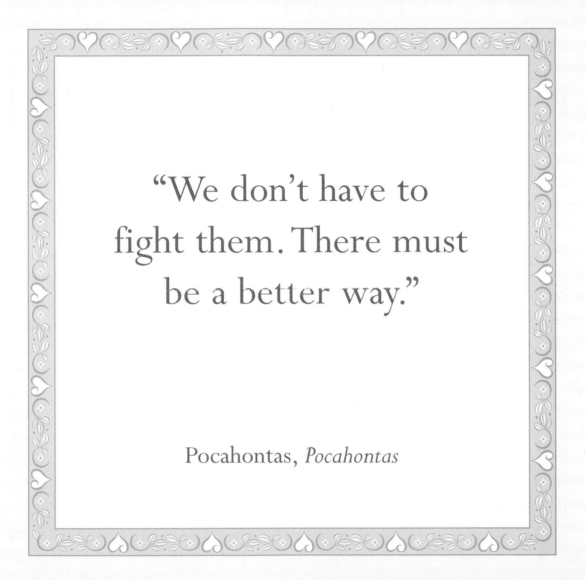

"We don't have to fight them. There must be a better way."

Pocahontas, *Pocahontas*

PRINCESS MAGIC

"Being brave
doesn't mean you go
looking for trouble."

Mufasa, *The Lion King*

PRINCESS MAGIC

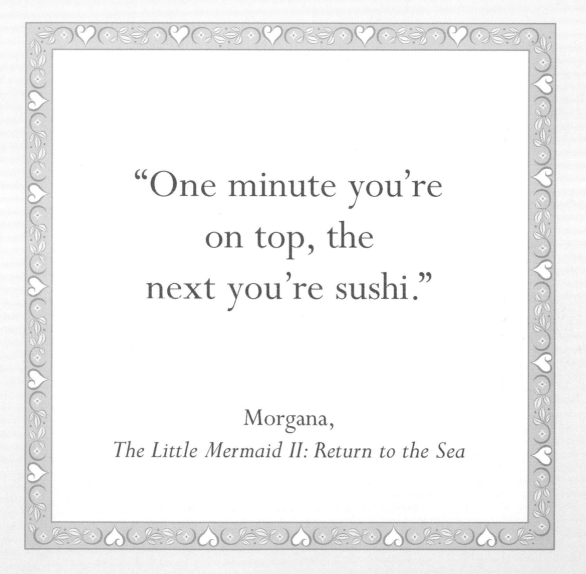

"One minute you're
on top, the
next you're sushi."

Morgana,
The Little Mermaid II: Return to the Sea

PRINCESS MAGIC

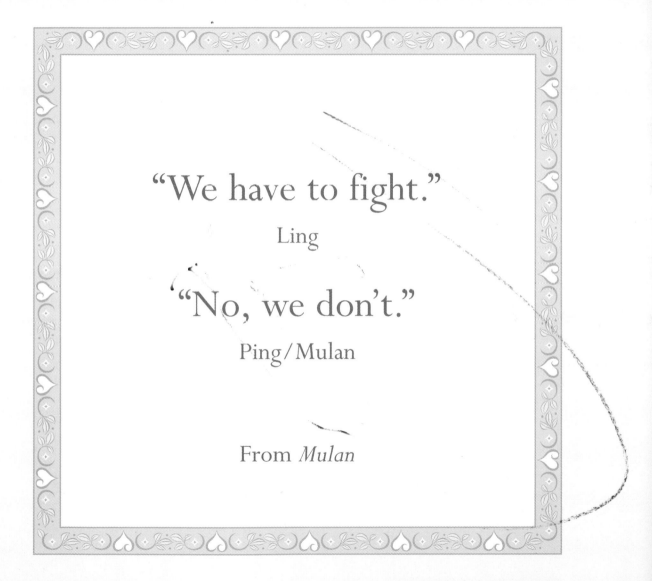

"We have to fight."

Ling

"No, we don't."

Ping/Mulan

From *Mulan*

GIVE PEACE A CHANCE

PRINCESS MAGIC

Lend
a
Hand

PRINCESS MAGIC

"Here you go."

Princess Jasmine, *Aladdin*

LEND A HAND

PRINCESS MAGIC

"Surprise!"

Mice, *Cinderella*

PRINCESS MAGIC

"Oh, we'll all pitch in."

Flora, *Sleeping Beauty*

LEND A HAND

PRINCESS MAGIC

"Do you trust me?"

Aladdin, *Aladdin*

LEND A HAND

PRINCESS MAGIC

"One good turn
deserves another."

The Doorknob, *Alice in Wonderland*

LEND A HAND

PRINCESS MAGIC

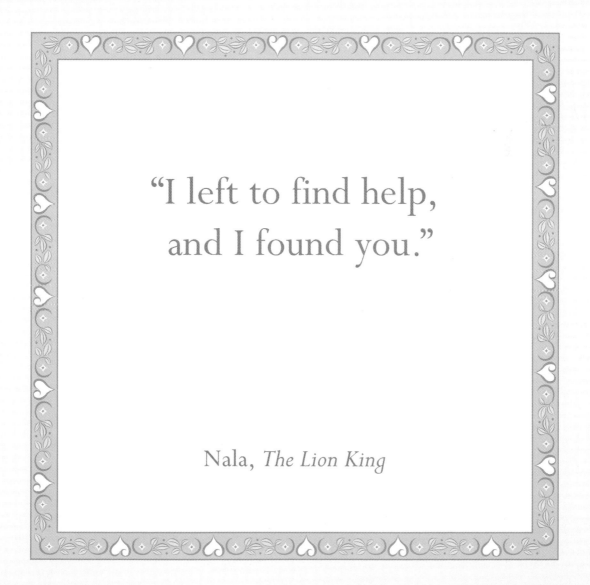

"I left to find help,
and I found you."

Nala, *The Lion King*

PRINCESS MAGIC

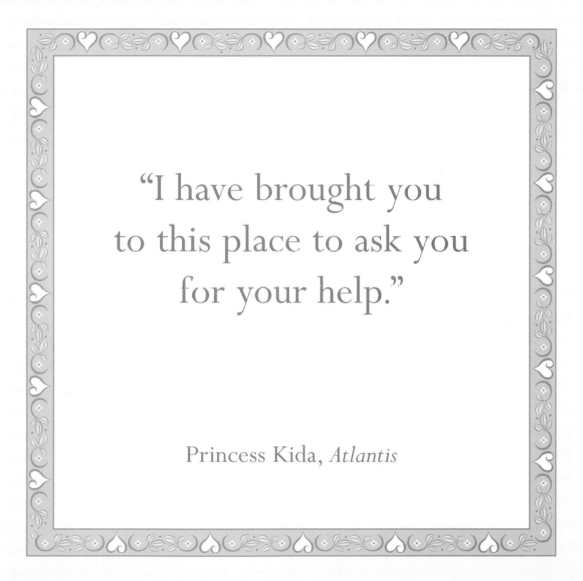

"I have brought you
to this place to ask you
for your help."

Princess Kida, *Atlantis*

PRINCESS MAGIC

Respect
Nature

PRINCESS MAGIC

"All around you are spirits, child. They live in the earth, the water, the sky. If you listen, they will guide you."

Grandmother Willow, *Pocahontas*

RESPECT NATURE

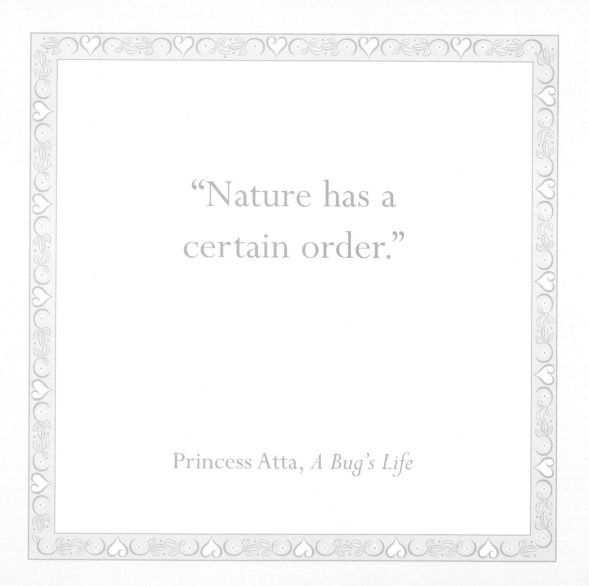

"Nature has a
certain order."

Princess Atta, *A Bug's Life*

PRINCESS MAGIC

"I'm giving you this locket so you will never forget that part of your heart will always belong to the sea."

King Triton,
The Little Mermaid II: Return to the Sea

RESPECT NATURE

PRINCESS MAGIC

"My, my. What beautiful blossoms we have this year. But, look, this one's late. But I'll bet that when it blooms, it will be the most beautiful of all."

Fa Zhou, *Mulan*

PRINCESS MAGIC

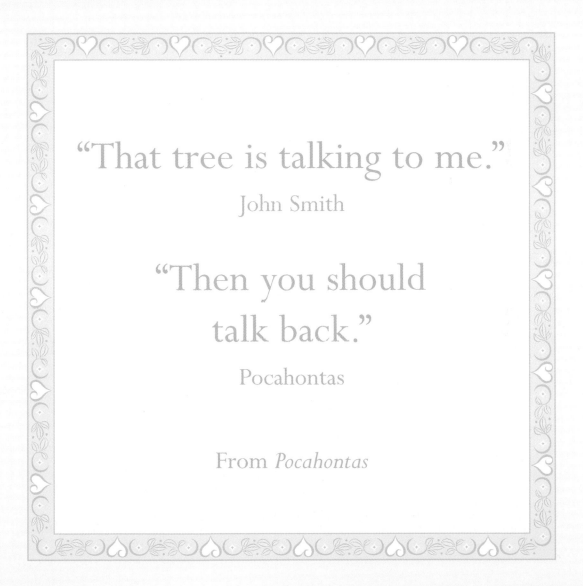

"That tree is talking to me."

John Smith

"Then you should
talk back."

Pocahontas

From *Pocahontas*

RESPECT NATURE

PRINCESS MAGIC

Anything's Possible!

PRINCESS MAGIC

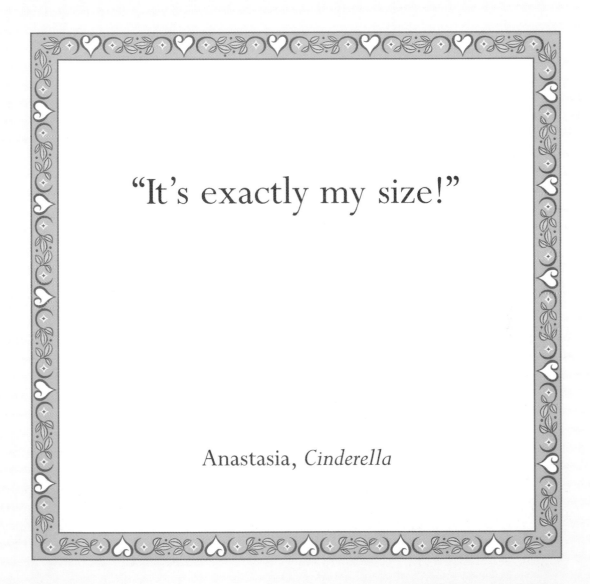

"It's exactly my size!"

Anastasia, *Cinderella*

PRINCESS MAGIC

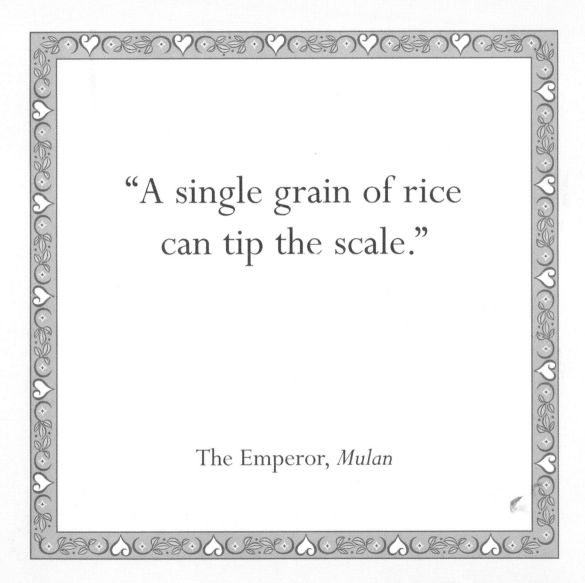

"A single grain of rice
can tip the scale."

The Emperor, *Mulan*

PRINCESS MAGIC

"Flowers can't talk."

Alice

"But of course we can,
my dear."

Rose

From *Alice in Wonderland*

PRINCESS MAGIC

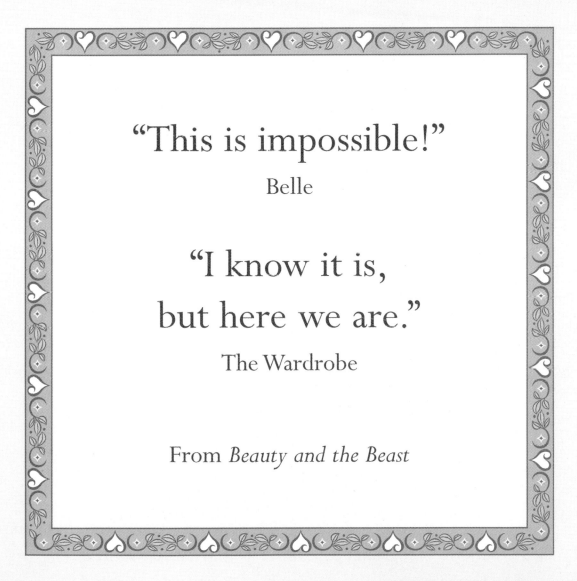

"This is impossible!"

Belle

"I know it is,
but here we are."

The Wardrobe

From *Beauty and the Beast*

PRINCESS MAGIC

"They say if you dream
a thing more than once,
it's sure to come true."

Briar Rose, *Sleeping Beauty*

PRINCESS MAGIC

Live
for
Today

PRINCESS MAGIC

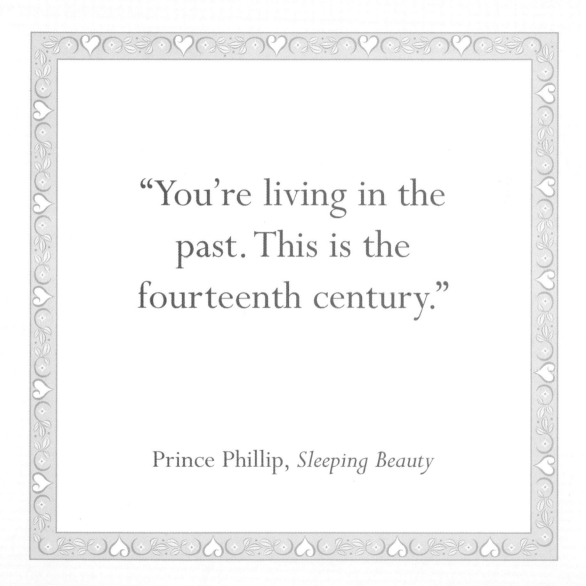

"You're living in the past. This is the fourteenth century."

Prince Phillip, *Sleeping Beauty*

PRINCESS MAGIC

"Come now, dry those tears. You can't go to the ball looking like that."

Fairy Godmother, *Cinderella*

LIVE FOR TODAY

PRINCESS MAGIC

"It's all so magical."

Princess Jasmine, *Aladdin*

LIVE FOR TODAY

PRINCESS MAGIC